Fairy Tales & Faith

Faith Lessons for a Real Happily Ever After

Antwan L. Houser Sr.
Illustrated by Courtney Smith

Cover and Interior Design: Derinda Babcock
Illustrations: Courtney Smith
Editor(s): Marcie Bridges, Deb Haggerty
Author Represented By: Cyle Young Literary Elites

PUBLISHED BY: Elk Lake Publishing, Inc., 35 Dogwood Drive, Plymouth, MA 02360, 2021

Library Cataloging Data
Names: Houser Sr., Antwan L. (Antwan L. Houser Sr.)
Fairytales & Faith / Antwan Houser
130 p. 21.6cm × 14cm (5.5in × 8.5 in.)
Identifiers: ISBN-13: 978-1-64949-134-3 (paperback) | 978-1-64949-135-0 (trade paperback) | 978-1-64949-136-7 (e-book)
Key Words: Devotional, inspirational, morality-building, middle grade, fairy tales, Scripture lessons, spiritual
LCCN: 2021930193 Fiction

DEDICATION

To my children:

Fairy Tales & Faith is dedicated to three of the greatest children a parent could ever ask for.

To my eldest and my firstborn son, Antwan Jr. (Aj)—you have turned into a fine young man that I am truly proud of. The sky is the limit for you, young man. Keep pushing and never give up.

To my baby girl, Bam Bam, Ms. Neah Simone, you are a beautiful young lady. Continue to be the best you can be and never let anyone stop you from accomplishing your dreams.

To my baby boy, my little bundle of joy, Ayce Logan (Affectionately known from his YouTube page as "Ayce in the Place"), who, at the time this book is being written, is two years old. Son, your personality and that smile of yours are going to take you far in life. As you grow older, continue to be a beacon of light and a ray of hope for those who meet you. You truly light up a room.

Lastly, to my beautiful wife, thank you for standing next to me through good and bad. You stood through the many long days and late nights of me working on this book, you've listened to the countless thoughts and ideas that flowed through my mind, and for that, I am grateful and thankful. I appreciate you and love you dearly. I thank God He placed you in my life.

May each of you put God first. Let Him guide you because if He be for you, He's more than the world against you. No one in this world can stop what God has for you. I am a proud father and love each of you to the utmost!

Thank you to all who will read this book and share the stories with your children. I pray these devotionals will help you, guide you, and propel you to a greater purpose. May the quotes be thought provoking and inspire you to want to be a better you. May the questions allow you to examine and self-reflect to become a tool that pushes you to reach your goals. May the fairy tales tap into the innocence of your childhood. Above all, my prayer is that God continue to smile down on you and your children, rewarding you with His blessings.

TABLE OF CONTENTS

You Are a Winner: The Tortoise and the Hare (Aesop)..........1

Who Do You Call?: Humpty Dumpty (Samuel Arnold)..........5

Things Are Not as Bad as They Seem: Jack and the Beanstalk (Joseph Jacobs)..........9

Nobody Can Have What's Yours: Cinderella (Charles Perrault)..........15

Hard Work Pays Off: The Three Little Pigs (Joseph Jacobs)..........21

You Are Beautiful: The Ugly Duckling (Hans Christian Andersen)..........25

Do Not Give Up: The Itsy Bitsy Spider (Iza Trapani)..........29

Put Others Above Yourself: The Tale of Two Brothers (A Jewish Story)..........33

You Can Overcome Your Obstacles: The Three Billy Goats Gruff (Peter Christen Asbjørnsen)39

It Is Okay to Speak: The Emperor's New Clothes (Hans Christian Andersen) 45

Prepare for Your Future: The Ant and Grasshopper:(Aesop)....................55

You Are Never a Loser: The Star Money (Dorothy Parker) 59

Do Not Be Fooled by the Enemy: The Wolf and Seven Young Goats (A Grimm Brothers Fairy Tale)........................63

Do Not Become Greedy: The Golden Goose (A Grimm Brothers Fairy Tale)...............71

Dangers of Arrogance: The Lion and The Gnat (Aesop) 81

Be Thankful for the Things You Do Have: The Travelers and the Plane Tree (Aesop) ..89

Entertaining Strangers: The Princess and The Pea (Hans Christian Andersen) 93

Not Everyone Is Who They Say They Are: The Quack Frog (Aesop)....................97

Follow the Leader: The Crab and His Mother (Aesop)........................101

Keep Your Eyes Open: The Lion and the Fox (Aesop)........................105

RESPECT OTHER'S PROPERTY: Goldilocks and
the Three Bears (Robert Southey)........109

BE SATISFIED WITH WHAT YOU HAVE: The Dog
and His Reflection (Aesop) 114

About the Author.....................119

FINISH
GREAT

DEVOTION 1: YOU ARE A WINNER

The Tale: The Tortoise and Hare

Long ago, a tortoise and a hare were walking together in the woods. The hare loved to tease the tortoise because he was so slow.

"Do you ever get anywhere?" Hare gazed down at the tortoise and laughed.

"Yes," Tortoise said, "and I bet I can run a race with you and win."

Hare smirked. He chuckled at the thought of running a race with Tortoise. But for fun, he agreed.

Fox, who was available, agreed to rule over the race. He marked the course, and with a shot, the runners raced. Hare had a fast start. Quick as a wink, he ran past the tortoise and out of sight. In fact, the hare got so far ahead he decided to rest in the grass.

"A quick nap won't hurt a thing," he said. "I'm so far ahead, I could tiptoe to the finish line and win."

So, he laid down in the cool grass and fell asleep.

All the while, Tortoise kept moving ahead, never stopping to rest. He walked on and soon he passed the spot where the hare lay sleeping in the shade.

Suddenly, Hare awoke from his nap. He looked down the path as far as he could see. Tortoise was nowhere in sight. He thought surely his competitor was still far, far behind. Hare thought he still had plenty of time to jog to the finish line before Tortoise.

As he stepped back onto the course, he saw Tortoise way in front of him, nearing the finish line. Shocked, Hare ran as hard and as fast as he could, but he had waited too long. The tortoise was so close he had reached the finish line before the hare.

The Moral:
Hare was much faster than Tortoise, but he allowed his focus to shift from the race to teasing the tortoise and taking a nap. Meanwhile, Tortoise kept moving forward, doing his best. You should always keep pushing yourself and run your best race even if someone is teasing you or if you are the underdog by a long shot. On the road of life, losing your focus can cause you to lose what you are supposed to win. Do not give up. We are already winners like Tortoise, if we keep our focus on the finish line and do our best.

The Happily Ever After:
"I have observed something else under the sun. The fastest runner doesn't always win the race, and the strongest warrior doesn't always win the battle. The wise sometimes go hungry, and the skillful are not necessarily wealthy. And those who are educated don't always lead successful lives. It is all decided

by chance, by being in the right place at the right time." (Ecclesiastes 9:11 NLT)

The Quest:
Lord, keep my focus on you. I know I can overcome if keep my eyes on you.

The Enchantment:
"The lesson is not in winning the race but comes in the preparation for the race."

The Once Upon A Time:
What have you learned?
Have you been in a similar situation?
How did you handle the situation?

Mirror, Mirror:
In the lines below, write one thing you can do this week to achieve a goal you have set for yourself?

TO THE KING
TRUTH
LIFE

DEVOTION 2: WHO DO YOU CALL?

The Tale: Humpty Dumpty

Once upon a time in a great walled kingdom lived Humpty Dumpty. He wanted to climb up and sit on the top of the city wall to see what he was missing.

What a great thing to see what lies on the other side, he thought to himself.

So, he scaled the wall. Once he reached the top, Humpty Dumpty tried to get comfortable, but he scooted a little too far to the edge and toppled right back down the wall to the ground below. SPLAT! What a sight—he broke into a thousand pieces!

"Sound the alarm! Humpty Dumpty has fallen!" The town crier ran through the streets. "Call all the king's horses! Call all the king's men! We've got to put Humpty Dumpty together again!"

They gathered in the town square. They worked hard to piece Humpty Dumpty back together, but all the king's horses and all the king's men could not put Humpty Dumpty back together again.

The Moral:
Through Humpty Dumpty's tale, we see an effort to repair a broken life. In Humpty's case, they called all the king's horses and all the king's men. When we fall and feel like we are broken beyond repair, the only one to call is the King of Kings. Nothing is too hard, and no one is too broken for God. He can heal our wounds and mend our brokenness.

The Happily Ever After:
"The LORD directs the steps of the godly. He delights in every detail of their lives. Though they stumble, they will never fall, for the LORD holds them by the hand." (Psalm 37:23–24 NLT)

The Quest:
Heavenly Father, please put my broken pieces back together so I can fulfill all you have for me to do in life. Amen.

The Enchantment:
"The fastest way to learn a life lesson is to fall, the more you fall the more you learn."

The Once Upon A Time:
When you fall in life, do you call on God?
Can you think of a time when things did not work out like you had hoped?
What did you learn?

Mirror, Mirror:

In the lines below, write about a time when you felt broken.

____

____

____

____

____

____

____

____

____

____

____

____

____

____

____

____

____

____

____

DEVOTION 3: THINGS ARE NOT AS BAD AS THEY SEEM

The Tale: Jack and the Beanstalk

A long time ago, a boy named Jack lived with his mother in the country. They were poor, living only on cow's milk because they had no food.

One day their cow could no longer produce milk. So, Jack's mother told him to take the animal to town and trade her for whatever he could get.

As Jack led the cow down the road, a voice called to him from the trees.

"Psst ... young man."

Jack glanced around but saw no one.

Then, a man stepped into his path.

"I'll trade you these magic beans I have in my hand for your cow."

Jack thought for a minute. Magic beans could grow many vegetables for my mom and me.

So, Jack agreed, and traded the cow. Thinking he had done a remarkable thing, he ran all the way home to tell his mother. But she was not happy about the magic beans and tossed them out the window.

"What will we eat? We have nothing left," she said, sending Jack to bed.

The next morning, Jack saw a big green leaf poking in through the window.

I bet the leaf grew from the magic beans, he thought.

Jack leaned his head from the window and gazed upward to behold the tall beanstalk stretching into the clouds. He stepped from the window and climbed up the stalk. He climbed so high he could no longer see the ground. At the top of the beanstalk, he followed a road that led to a big castle.

Jack entered the castle and walked into the kitchen where a giant woman was cooking.

"Where did you come from?" she asked. "What's your name?"

"My name is Jack. I climbed up a beanstalk."

The woman gave Jack something to eat and told him to leave before her husband came home.

"He eats children." she warned.

Before Jack could leave, the giant returned. The woman told Jack to hide in the oven.

The giant opened the front door of his castle and slammed it shut.

"Fee Fi Fo Fum—I smell the blood of an Englishman!" the giant said.

The giant's wife told him there were no children there.

So, the giant ate and then, took a nap after lunch. Jack jumped out of the oven, grabbed a bag of gold, and ran to the beanstalk as fast as he could. Down, down, down he climbed until he was back at home, safe.

The next day, Jack climbed the beanstalk again. This time he returned home with the giant's harp that played pretty music.

On the third day, Jack climbed the beanstalk and grabbed a chicken that laid golden eggs, but the chicken started to cackle and woke the giant.

THUMP, THUMP, THUMP. The giant chased Jack to the beanstalk. He climbed down the stalk after Jack.

Jack hurried to the bottom of the beanstalk and chopped it down with an axe.

The giant came crashing down with a loud THUD.

Jack bought his cow back and lived happily ever after on the farm with his mother.

The Moral:

In this fairy tale, Jack's mother was not happy with the trade. She was so mad at Jack she threw the beans out of the window. Jack was probably upset because he thought he made a good decision, but he knew the beans were thrown to the ground. Yet, the next day they grew. We all do things in life that not everyone thinks is best but, even in those times if our seed is planted in God, it can still grow.

The Happily Ever After:

"And God will generously provide all you need. Then you will always have everything you need and plenty left over to share with others." (2 Corinthians 9:8, NLT)

The Quest:

Thank you, God, for the good seeds deposited in my life. Help me to take what I have and plant good seeds in others so they might grow to know you.

The Enchantment:

"Growth comes from growing others."

The Once Upon A Time:

Have you ever been in a situation where you felt like no one understood you or what you were trying to do?

How did that make you feel?

What are some areas in your life where you would like to see some growth?

Mirror Mirror:

Notes, takeaway, and personal reflections you gained from the lesson.

____

____

____

____

____

____

DEVOTION 4: NOBODY CAN HAVE WHAT'S YOURS

The Tale: Cinderella

Once upon a time, a beautiful girl named Cinderella lived in an old castle with a wicked stepmother and two ugly stepsisters. The wicked stepmother and ugly stepsisters were very jealous of Cinderella and made her work all day and night—cleaning, cooking, and washing the clothes.

One day, she overheard her stepmother and stepsisters discussing an upcoming royal ball at the palace.

"Cinderella, dear, get our ball gowns ready. We are going to a party," the wicked stepmother said.

Cinderella hurried to help them dress. As she watched the carriage take them away to the palace, Cinderella cried. Just then, a bright ball of light floated into the room.

"Cinderella, I'm your fairy godmother. Don't be afraid, my dear. I'm going to help you get ready for the ball."

"I'm not going to the ball. I have nothing to wear and no way to get there."

"Nonsense. Now stand back and watch this." With a wave of her wand—POOF—Cinderella wore the most beautiful dress ever seen. And to finish her look, the fairy godmother put glass slippers on Cinderella's feet. They fit her feet perfectly.

The fairy godmother waved her wand again and turned a big pumpkin into a beautiful carriage. She turned two mice into strong horses to pull the carriage and another two became footmen.

The fairy godmother warned Cinderella, "Return before midnight. As soon the clock strikes twelve, everything will go back to the way it was."

Cinderella promised to return in time as she climbed into the carriage. Away she went through the forest to the royal palace. She could hardly believe her eyes. She could hear the most wonderful music playing.

She danced with every young man at the ball, until one young man asked Cinderella to dance with him the rest of the night. Being swept up in the music, she forgot to watch the time.

Soon the clock struck twelve—BONG! BONG! BONG! Cinderella suddenly remembered the fairy godmother's words. She ran away from the handsome young man. She had to run all the way back home because her carriage had turned back into a pumpkin. But one of her shoes fell off when she ran out of the palace.

The next day, three men on horses rode up to the castle where Cinderella lived. "We are here to find the owner of this glass slipper." They ordered each girl to try on the shoe.

The wicked stepmother was the first one to try it on. She stuffed her long narrow foot in as far as it would go, but the shoe shot across the room as fast as she put it on.

The two ugly stepsisters also tried, but they couldn't get their big feet in the small shoe.

The men were about to leave when they saw Cinderella peeking around a corner.

Cinderella slipped her foot right into the shoe for a perfect fit.

The wicked stepmother gasped and held her chest. One of the ugly stepsisters cried and nearly fainted on the steps while the other frowned.

At last, Prince Charming had found Cinderella. She rode away with him and they lived happily ever after.

The Moral:
In this tale, the prince searched all over for the owner of the shoe, but the shoe only fit Cinderella. God designed your life, and He has blessings that have your name on them. Those blessings have a purpose for you. Like in this tale, people will attempt to block you from receiving what God has for you, but if something has been designed for you, no one else will be able to own it. Since the shoe fits, wear it.

The Happily Ever After:
"So humble yourselves under the mighty power of God, and at the right time he will lift you up in

honor. Give all your worries and cares to God, for he cares about you." (1 Peter 5:6–7 NLT)

The Quest:
Heavenly Father, thank you for the blessings and things you have already granted me. As I go through my week, please remind me that no one can take what you have planned for my life.

The Enchantment:
"Custom fit only looks good on the one whom it was fitted for."

The Once Upon A Time:
Have you ever had someone bully you?
How did you handle the situation?
Have you ever worried that someone or something could stop the plans God has for your life?

Mirror Mirror:
Notes, takeaway, and personal reflections you gained from the lesson.

____

____

____

____

____

____

DEVOTION 5: HARD WORK PAYS OFF

The Tale: The Three Little Pigs

Once upon a time, there were three little pigs. One pig built a house of straw while the second pig built his house with sticks. They built their houses very quickly and then, sang and danced all day because they were lazy. The third little pig worked hard all day and built his house with bricks.

A big bad wolf saw the two little pigs while they danced and played, and he thought, what juicy tender meals they will make. He chased the two pigs, and they ran and hid in their houses.

The big bad wolf went to the first house. He huffed and puffed and blew the straw house down. The frightened little pig ran to the second pig's house made of sticks.

The big bad wolf came to the second house. He huffed and puffed and blew the stick house down too.

Now, the two little pigs were terrified and ran to the third pig's house made of bricks. The big bad wolf tried to huff and puff and blow the house down, but he could not because the house was well built, and the little pigs were safe inside.

The Moral:

Hard work pays off. While the pig who built a brick house worked hard, the other two pigs goofed off. The pig who built the brick house could have joined them. However, he chose to make sure his house would stand the huffs and puffs of the wolf. To get where you want to be in life, sometimes you will need to work harder than everyone else. Do not get discouraged if you find yourself working harder than others. Oftentimes, your outcome is better than those who took the easy route.

The Happily Ever After:

"But someone who does not know, and then does something wrong, will be punished only lightly. When someone has been given much, much will be required in return; and when someone has been entrusted with much, even more will be required." (Luke 12:48 NLT)

The Quest:

As I go through life, please give me the ability to work hard and complete the tasks, which are set before me. Though it may be hard, I ask you for endurance to see things through.

The Enchantment:

"Working hard can be hard and requires hard work, Life can be hard and requires even harder work."

The Once Upon A Time:
Have you ever felt you had to work harder than everyone else at something?
How did you handle the situation?
Have you ever built something in a lazy way?

Mirror Mirror:
Notes, takeaway, and personal reflections you gained from the lesson.

____

____

____

____

____

____

____

____

____

____

____

____

____

____

____

DEVOTION 6: YOU ARE BEAUTIFUL

The Tale: The Ugly Duckling

On a beautiful summer day, the sun shined warmly on an old house near a river. Behind the house, a mother duck sat on ten eggs. . One by one all the eggs broke open. All except one, which was the biggest egg of all. Mother duck sat all day on the big egg. At last, it broke open. !

Out jumped the last baby duck. It looked big and strong, but it was gray and ugly.

The next day mother duck took all her little ducks to the river. She jumped into it. All her baby ducks jumped in. The big ugly duckling jumped in too.

They swam and played together. The ugly duckling swam better than the other ducklings.

"Quack, quack! Come with me to the farmyard," said mother duck to her baby ducks who followed her.

The farmyard is very noisy, the poor duckling thought. The hens peck me, the rooster flies at me, the ducks bite me, and the farmer kicks me.

He decided to run away. He came to a river and saw many big, beautiful birds swimming in the water. Their feathers were so white, their necks so long, their wings so pretty. The little duckling gazed at them. He wanted to stay and watch them. He knew they were swans and he wanted to be beautiful like them.

Winter came. Everything was white with snow. Ice covered the river and the ugly duckling shivered and frowned.

Spring arrived. The sun shined warm rays. The land was fresh and green.

One morning the ugly duckling saw the beautiful swans again. He knew them and wanted to swim with them in the river, but he was afraid of them. He wanted to die. So, he ran into the river. When he looked in the water, he saw a beautiful swan. It was he! He was no more an ugly duckling. He was a beautiful white swan.

The Moral:
Teasing hurts people. The ugly duckling was unhappy because he didn't fit in. The other animals bullied the poor duckling, not knowing who he was or who he would become because they looked at him on the outside. True beauty is on the inside.

The Happily Ever After:
"Thank you for making me so wonderfully complex! Your workmanship is marvelous—how well I know it." (Psalm 139:14 NLT)

The Quest:
Heavenly Father, as I go through life, please help me to see others as you see them.

The Enchantment:
"True beauty is on the inside."

The Once Upon A Time:
What have you learned:
Have you been in a similar situation?
How did you handle the situation?
Does it align with the moral? How?

Mirror Mirror:
Notes, takeaway, and personal reflections you gained from the lesson. ______________________

____

____

____

____

____

____

____

____

____

DEVOTION 7: DO NOT GIVE UP

The Tale: The Itsy Bitsy Spider

The itsy bitsy spider climbed up the waterspout.
Down came the rain and washed the spider out.
Out came the sun and dried up all the rain.
So, the itsy bitsy spider climbed up the spout again

The Moral:
Life is filled with difficulties that either enable us or disable us. Do not be dismayed. After the rain the sun will shine, and like the itsy bitsy spider we can climb again.

The Happily Ever After:
"So let's not get tired of doing what is good. At just the right time we will reap a harvest of blessing if we don't give up." (Galatians 6:9 NLT)

The Quest:
As I experience storms in my life, allow me to endure knowing you may have a message or a test

in the rain. I thank you for the rain as it gives me appreciation for the sun.

The Enchantment:
"Patience is key. Giving up to quickly only delays you reaching your goal."

The Once Upon A Time:
Have you been in a similar situation?
How did you handle the situation?
What have you learned?

Mirror Mirror:
Notes, takeaway, and personal reflections you gained from the lesson. ______________________

____

____

____

____

____

____

____

____

____

____

DEVOTION 8: PUTTING OTHERS ABOVE YOURSELF

The Tale: The Tale of Two Brothers

Long ago, two brothers inherited their father's land. The two brothers divided the land in half and each one farmed his own section. Over time, the older brother married and had six children, while the younger brother never married.

One night, the younger brother lay awake. "It's not fair that each of us has half the land to farm," he thought. "My brother has six children to feed and I have none. He should have more grain than I do."

So that night the younger brother went to his silo, gathered a large bundle of wheat, and climbed the hill separating the two farms and traveled over to his brother's farm. Leaving the wheat in his brother's silo, the younger brother returned home, feeling pleased with himself.

Earlier that very same night, the older brother also laid awake. "It's not fair that each of us has half the land to farm," he thought. "In my old age, my wife and I will have our grown children to take care of us—not to mention grandchildren—while my brother will probably have none. If he sells more grain from the fields now, he can provide for himself with dignity in his old age."

So that night, too, he secretly gathered a large bundle of wheat, climbed the hill, left it in his brother's silo, and returned home, feeling pleased with himself.

The next morning, the younger brother was surprised to see the amount of grain in his barn unchanged. "I must not have taken as much wheat as I thought," he said, bemused. "Tonight, I'll be sure to take more."

That very same moment, his older brother was also standing in his barn, musing the same thoughts.

After night fell, each brother gathered a greater amount of wheat from his barn and in the dark, secretly delivered it to his brother's barn. The next morning, the brothers stood in their barns, perplexed.

"How can I be mistaken?" each one scratched his head. "There's the same amount of grain here as there was before I cleared the pile for my brother. This is impossible! Tonight, I'll make no mistake. I'll take the pile down to the very floor. That way, I'll be sure the grain gets delivered to my brother."

The third night, more determined than ever, each brother gathered a large pile of wheat from his barn, loaded it onto a cart, and slowly pulled his haul through the fields and up the hill to his brother's barn. At the top of the hill, under the shadow of a moon, each brother noticed a figure approaching. Who could it be?

When the two brothers recognized the form of the other brother and the load he was pulling behind, they realized what had happened. Without a word, they dropped the ropes to their carts and embraced.

The Moral:

We should always think about others over ourselves. If we have more than we need, we should share. Many people in the world are less fortunate and do not have many things that we have. How do you think they would feel if we shared with them? What if we were in need, would we want someone to share with us? Like these two brothers, each one thought enough of the other to put aside himself to help the other succeed. God blesses us to be a blessing. He loves when we share with one another.

The Happily Ever After:

"The man answered, 'You must love the LORD your God with all your heart, all your soul, all your strength, and all your mind. And, love your neighbor as yourself.'" (Luke 10:27 NLT)

The Quest:

Lord, thank you for supplying my needs and always being there for me. Help me to likewise follow your example and be a help to others that are in need.

The Enchantment:
"More than, is more than someone else's need."

The Once Upon A Time:
What have you learned?
Have you been in a similar situation?
How did you handle the situation?

Mirror Mirror:
Notes, takeaway, and personal reflections you gained from the lesson.

____

____

____

____

____

____

____

____

____

____

____

____

____

____

____

____

____

____

____

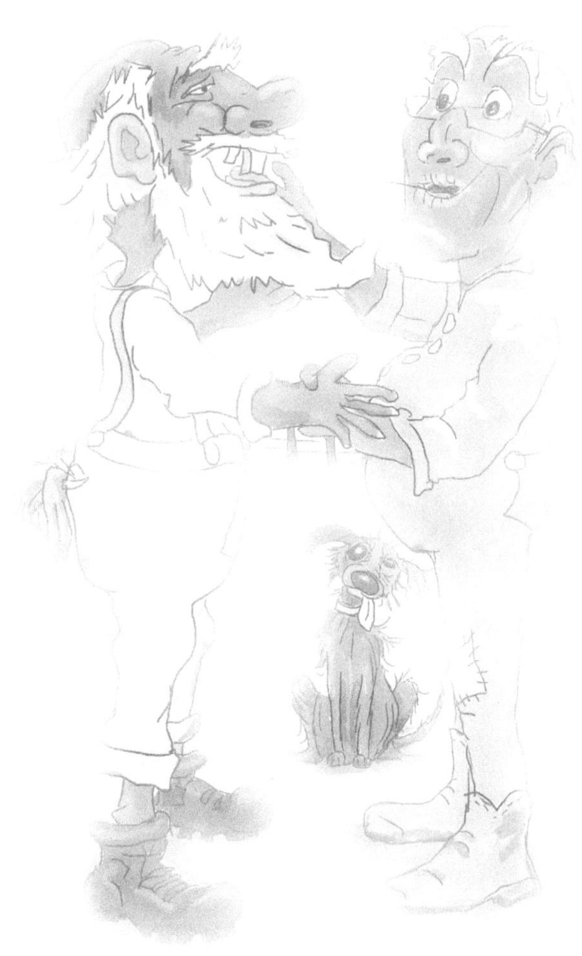

DEVOTION 9: YOU CAN OVERCOME YOUR OBSTACLES

Once upon a time there were three billy goats named Gruff, who wanted to travel up a hillside to make themselves fat.

On the way up, they had to cross a bridge over a cascading stream. Under the bridge lived a mean, ugly troll with big eyes and a long nose.

First, the youngest billy goat Gruff began to cross the bridge.

TRIP, TRAP, TRIP, TRAP

"Who's that tripping over my bridge?" roared the troll.

"Oh, it is only I, the tiniest billy goat Gruff, and I'm going up to the hillside to make myself fat," said the billy goat, with a small voice.

"Now, I'm coming to gobble you up," said the troll.

"Oh, no! Pray don't take me. I'm too little, that I am," said the billy goat. "Wait a bit till the second billy goat Gruff comes. He's much bigger."

"Well, be off with you," said the troll.

A little while later came the second billy goat Gruff to cross the bridge.

TRIP, TRAP, TRIP, TRAP, TRIP, TRAP

"Who's that tripping over my bridge?" roared the troll.

"Oh, it's the second billy goat Gruff, and I'm going up to the hillside to make myself fat," said the billy goat, who hadn't such a small voice.

"Now I'm coming to gobble you up," said the troll.

"Oh, no! Don't take me. Wait a little till the big billy goat Gruff comes. He's much bigger."

"Very well! Be off with you," said the troll.

But just then up came the big billy goat Gruff.

TRIP, TRAP, TRIP, TRAP, TRIP, TRAP

This billy goat was so heavy that the bridge creaked and groaned under him.

"Who's that tramping over my bridge?" roared the troll.

"It's I! The big billy goat Gruff," said the billy goat, who had a booming voice of his own.

"Now I'm coming to gobble you up," roared the troll.

Well, come along! I've got two spears,
And I'll poke your ears.
Besides, I've got two stones,
And I'll sling them to break your bones.

That was what the big billy goat said. And then he jumped on the troll, and poked him, and tossed him into the cascade. Then, he returned to the hillside where the billy goats fattened up.

The Moral:
The three billy goats met a mean troll who wanted to eat them. Through wisdom, the billy goats crossed the bridge. No matter what you do, you will have obstacles. Not all obstacles will cause you to fail. Some may test your will. Some may test your endurance. Do we really want the goal we are trying to reach? With God as our light, we do not have to fear obstacles. We can cross bridges knowing God has a plan, and He is bigger than any obstacle standing in our way.

The Happily Ever After:
"The LORD is my light and my salvation— so why should I be afraid? The LORD is my fortress, protecting me from danger, so why should I tremble?" (Psalms 27:1 NLT)

The Quest:
Lord, as I encounter obstacles in my life please give me the strength to overcome and help me to see the lesson in the midst of the obstacle.

The Enchantment:
"Fear itself is an obstacle that we must overcome, to overcome."

The Once Upon A Time:
What have you learned?
Have you been in a similar situation?
How did you handle the situation?

Mirror Mirror:

Notes, takeaway, and personal reflections you gained from the lesson.

____

____

____

____

____

____

____

____

____

____

____

____

____

____

____

____

____

____

____

____

____

____

____

DEVOTION 10: IT IS OKAY TO SPEAK UP

The Tale: The Emperor's New Clothes

Many, many years ago lived an emperor, who loved new clothes, so he spent all his money to buy them. His only ambition was to always dress well. He did not care for his soldiers nor did he care about ruling. The only thing he thought to do was to show himself off with new clothes as often as possible. He had a coat for every hour of the day. As often as you would say of a normal king "He is busy ruling the kingdom," you could say of him, "The emperor is in his dressing room trying on new gear."

The great city where he lived was a very busy place, every day many strangers from all parts of the globe arrived. One day, two swindlers arrived and told everyone they were weavers. They said they could make the finest cloth anyone could imagine. Their colors and patterns, they said, were not only very beautiful, but were made of a special material invisible to fools.

That must be wonderful cloth, thought the emperor. If I were dressed in a suit made of this cloth, I would know which people are fools in my kingdom and therefore, should not hold their jobs. I must have this cloth made for me without delay.

And he gave a large sum of money to those rascals, in advance, so that they should get to work immediately. The men set up two looms and pretended to work hard. They asked for the finest silk and the most precious gold cloth. All the expensive material they got they hid away for themselves and worked at the empty looms till late at night.

I'd love to know how they are getting on with the cloth, thought the emperor. But he felt worried when he remembered that anyone who could not see the beautiful materials was a fool. Of course, he thought he would be able to see the cloth, but he decided to send someone else first to check it out, just in case. Everybody in town knew how remarkable the clothes were and were dying to discover how foolish their neighbors were.

I shall send my honest old minister to the weavers, thought the emperor. He can see how fabric looks, for he is very clever.

The good old minister went into the room where the swindlers sat before the empty looms. Goodness gracious, he thought as he opened his eyes wide, I cannot see anything at all, but he did not say so. Both swindlers told him to come near and asked him if he admired the lovely pattern and the beautiful colors, pointing to the empty looms. The poor old minister tried his best, but he could see nothing, for there was nothing to be seen.

Oh dear, he thought, am I a fool? I would never have thought so, but nobody must find out! Is it possible that I am too foolish to do my job? No, I cannot admit I was not able to see the cloth.

"Have you got nothing to say?" said one of the swindlers, while he pretended to be busy weaving.

"Oh, it is very pretty, really beautiful," replied the old minister peering through his glasses. "What a beautiful pattern, what brilliant colors! I will tell the emperor I like the cloth very much."

"We are pleased to hear that," said the two weavers, and they described to him the colors and explained the curious pattern. The old minister listened carefully, so he would be able to tell the emperor what they said, and so he did tell him.

Now the swindlers asked for more money, silk and gold cloth, which they said they required for weaving. They kept everything for themselves and not a thread came near the loom, but they continued, as before, to pretend to work at the empty looms.

Soon afterwards, the emperor sent another good man to the weavers to see how they were doing, and if the cloth was nearly finished. Like the old minister, he studied the looms but could see nothing, as there was nothing to be seen.

"Is it not a beautiful piece of cloth?" asked the two rascals, showing and explaining the fantastic pattern, which, however, did not exist.

I think I am not a fool, thought the man. Maybe I am not clever enough for my job. I must not let anyone know, and he praised the cloth, which he did not see and praised the beautiful colors and the fine pattern. "It is very excellent," he said to the emperor.

Everybody in the whole town talked about the precious cloth. At last, the emperor wished to see it himself—while it was still on the loom. With several assistants, including the two who had already been there, he visited the two swindlers, who now worked as hard as they could, but without using any thread.

"Is it not magnificent?" said the two old men who had been there before. "Your Majesty must admire the colors and the pattern." And then, they pointed to the empty looms, for they expected that the others could see the cloth.

I do not see anything at all, thought the emperor. What is this? Am I a fool? Too foolish to be an emperor? That would indeed be the most terrible thing that could happen to me.

"Really," he said, turning to the weavers, "your cloth is wonderful, really wonderful." He nodded as he gazed at the empty loom, because he did not want to say that he could not see anything.

All his attendants, who were with him, gawked and gazed, and although they could not see anything more than the others, they repeated the emperor, "It is very beautiful."

Now all of them advised him to wear the new magnificent clothes at the great procession which would soon take place.

"It is magnificent, beautiful, excellent," they said.

Everybody seemed delighted, and the emperor appointed the two swindlers as Imperial Court weavers.

The whole night before the day of the procession, these two clever rascals pretended to work, and burned more than sixteen candles. They wanted people to see that they were busy finishing the emperor's new clothes. They pretended to take the cloth from the loom, and worked about in the air with big scissors, and they sewed needles without thread. At last, they said, "The emperor's new clothes are ready now."

The emperor and all his barons then approached the hall. The swindlers held their arms up as if they held something in their hands and said, "These are the trousers!" "This is the coat!" and "Here is the cloak!" and so on. "They are all as light as a cobweb, so light in fact, it feels as if you have nothing on at all, but that is just the beauty of the clothes."

"Indeed!" said all the assistants, but they could not see anything, for there was nothing to be seen.

"Does it please your Majesty now to undress," said the swindlers, "that we may help your Majesty in putting on the new suit in front of the mirror?"

The emperor undressed and the swindlers pretended to put the new suit on him, one piece after another. The emperor observed himself in the glass from all sides.

But his court praised the garments—that did not, however, exist.

"How well they look!"

"How well they fit!"

"What a beautiful pattern!"

"What fine colors!"

"That is a magnificent suit of clothes!"

Then, someone announced it was time to start the procession.

"I am ready," said the emperor. "Does not my suit fit me wonderfully?" Then, he turned once more to the looking glass, so people would think he was admiring his clothes again.

Two boys were ready to walk behind the emperor, to hold up the train of the emperor's clothes—that is, the material from his clothes that would have otherwise trailed behind on the ground. They stretched their hands downward as if to lift the train and pretend to hold something in their hands. They did not want people to know they could not see or feel anything.

The emperor marched in the procession under a beautiful canopy and all who saw him in the street and out of the windows exclaimed, "Indeed, the emperor's new suit is amazing! What a long train he has! How well it fits him!"

Nobody wanted to admit they saw nothing, for then, it would mean they were too foolish. Never were the emperor's clothes more admired.

At last, a little boy piped up, "But he has nothing on at all! He's completely nude!"

"Good Heavens! I'm so sorry about that," said the embarrassed father. "He's just a simple boy who doesn't know any better." But soon, the whole crowd whispered what the child had said.

"He does not have anything on at all!" cried all the people, realizing the truth.

The emperor suddenly realized they were right, but he thought to himself, I must keep pretending until the end or I'll look even more foolish.

So, the emperor tried to walk with even greater dignity, while the crowd laughed and teased him all the way. Afterwards, he sent his soldiers to arrest the two swindlers, but they had fled the city with all the money and precious material.

For the rest of his days, people joked about the time the emperor went for a parade with no clothes on, and he never lived it down.

The Moral:
This emperor walked around with no clothes on because he was convinced he had real clothes on. No one decided to speak up and tell him because they did not want to look like a fool. Someday, you will need to speak up even when no one else will. Speaking up especially when something is not right does not make you stupid or uncool. Speaking up can stop embarrassment or become a teachable moment. It is better to speak up then to remain silent when things feel wrong.

The Happily Ever After:
"The tongue can bring death or life; those who love to talk will reap the consequences." (Proverbs 18:21 NLT)

The Quest:
Heavenly Father, I ask you to give me courage and put the right words in my mouth to speak up when needed.

The Enchantment:
"Never close your mouth to something that can be used to save something or someone." .

The Once Upon A Time:
What have you learned?
Have you been in a similar situation?
How did you handle the situation?

Mirror, Mirror:
Write personal reflections you gained from the lesson.

____

____

____

____

____

____

____

____

____

____

____

____

DEVOTION 11: PREPARE FOR YOUR FUTURE

The Tale: The Ant and Grasshopper

One bright day in late autumn, a family of ants bustled about in the warm sunshine to dry out the grain they had stored up during the summer. A starving grasshopper, his fiddle under his arm, trotted up and humbly begged for a bite to eat.

"What!" cried the ants in surprise, "haven't you stored anything away for the winter? What in the world were you doing all last summer?"

"I didn't have time to store up any food," whined the grasshopper, "I was so busy making music that before I knew it the summer was gone."

The ants shrugged their shoulders in disgust.

"Making music, were you?" they cried. "Very well, now dance!" And they turned their backs on the grasshopper and went on with their work.

The Moral:
If we get caught up in the moment, we can miss what is most important. The grasshopper spent

his time playing his fiddle and making music but did not prepare for his future. As God's children, we will spend eternal life in victory with the Lord. Distractions will come our way to divert us from important things, and we may be good at and enjoy doing them. But in life, we must not stop preparing for our final home in Heaven that God has prepared for us.

The Happily Ever After:
"There is more than enough room in my Father's home. If this were not so, would I have told you that I am going to prepare a place for you? When everything is ready, I will come and get you, so that you will always be with me where I am." (John 14:2–3 NLT)

The Quest:
Lord, guide me in the way I should go and keep my eyes on you.

The Enchantment:
"A future without a plan and preparation to get there is a dream that means nothing."

The Once Upon A Time:
What have you learned?
How are you preparing for your future?
What plan do you have in place to achieve it?

Mirror, Mirror:

Notes, takeaway, and personal reflections you gained from the lesson.

DEVOTION 12: YOU ARE NEVER A LOSER

The Tale: The Star Money

There was once a little girl whose father and mother had perished. She was so poor she no longer had a home to live in or a bed to sleep in. At last, she had nothing else but the clothes she wore and a bit of bread in her hand, which some charitable soul had given her. She was, however, a good child and pious. Yet forsaken, she went forth into the open country, trusting the good God.

Then, a poor man met her, who said: "Ah, give me something to eat, I am so hungry!"

She gave him all her bread, and said, "May God bless it for your use," and went onward.

Then, came a child who moaned and said, "My head is so cold, give me something to cover it with."

So, she took off her hood and gave it to him, and when she walked a little farther, she met another child who had no jacket and shivered with cold. Then, she gave up her own.

A little farther on, one begged for a frock—and she gave that away also.

At dark, she entered a forest, and there came yet another child who asked for a little shirt, and the good little girl thought to herself, "It is a dark night, and no one sees me, I can give my shirt." So, she took it off, and gave that away also.

And as she stood having not one single thing left, suddenly some stars from heaven fell. Yet, they were nothing else but hard smooth pieces of money. Moreover, although she had just given her little shirt away, she wore a new tunic which was of the very finest linen. Then, she gathered the money into the pocket of her new robe and was rich all the days of her life.

The Moral:

When we are willing to help others unselfishly, we receive the greatest from God. In this story, this little girl met several needy strangers. Instead of turning them away, she gave all she had. When we encounter someone in need, we should have a willing attitude to do the same. We must humble ourselves and not miss an opportunity to help them. God may have sent the person we met to give us a charitable opportunity.

The Happily Ever After:

"'For I was hungry, and you fed me. I was thirsty, and you gave me a drink. I was a stranger, and you invited me into your home. I was naked, and you gave me clothing. I was sick, and you cared for me.

I was in prison, and you visited me.' Then these righteous ones will reply, 'Lord, when did we ever see you hungry and feed you? Or thirsty and give you something to drink? Or a stranger and show you hospitality? Or naked and give you clothing? When did we ever see you sick or in prison and visit you?' And the King will say, 'I tell you the truth, when you did it to one of the least of these my brothers and sisters, you were doing it to me!'" (Matthew 25:35–40 NLT)

The Quest:
Lord, keep my focus on you. I know I can overcome if keep my eyes on you.

The Enchantment:
"A true winner never loses even when they lose."

The Once Upon A Time:
What have you learned?
Have you been in a similar situation?
How did you handle the situation?

Mirror, Mirror:
In the lines below, write one thing you can do this week to achieve a goal you have set for yourself?

____

____

____

DEVOTION 13: DO NOT BE FOOLED BY THE ENEMY

The Tale: The Wolf and Seven Young Goats

Once upon a time an old goat had seven little kids and loved them with all the love of a mother for her children. One day she decided to go to the forest and fetch food. So she called all seven to her and said, "Dear children, I have to go into the forest, be on your guard against the wolf, if he comes in, he will devour you all, every bit. The wretch often disguises himself, but you will know him at once by his rough voice and his black paws."

The kids said, "Dear mother, we will care for ourselves, you may go away without any anxiety." Then, the old one bleated, and went on her way with an easy mind.

It was not long before someone knocked at the house door and called, "Open the door, dear kids, your mother is here, and has brought something back with her for each of you." But the little kids knew it was the wolf, by the rough voice.

"We will not open the door," cried they, "you are not our mother. She has a soft, pleasant voice, but your voice is rough, you are the wolf."

Then, the wolf went away to a shopkeeper and bought himself a great lump of chalk to eat and made his voice soft with it. Then, he returned, knocked at the door of the house, and called, "Open the door, dear kids, your mother is here and has brought something back with her for each of you."

But the wolf had laid his black paws against the window, and the kids saw them and cried, "We will not open the door, our mother does not have black paws like you, you are the wolf."

Then, the wolf ran to a baker and said, "I have hurt my paws, rub some dough over them for me." And when the baker had rubbed his paws over, he ran to the miller and said, "Strew some white meal over my paws for me." The miller thought to himself, the wolf wants to deceive someone, and refused, but the wolf said, "If you will not do it, I will devour you." Then, the miller was afraid, and made his paws white for him.

Now the wretch went for the third time to the house, knocked on the door and said, "Open the door for me, kids, your dear little mother has come home, and has brought every one of you something back from the forest with her."

The little kids cried, "First show us your paws that we may know if you are our dear little mother."

Then, he put his paws in through the window, and when the kids saw they were white, they believed he told the truth, and opened the door. But who should come in but—the wolf. The terrified kids ran and hid. One sprang under the table, the second into the bed, the third into the stove, the fourth into the kitchen, the fifth into the cupboard, the sixth under the washing bowl, and the seventh into the clock case. But the wolf found them all, and used no great ceremony, one after the other he swallowed them down. The youngest, who was in the clock case, was the only one he did not find. When the wolf had satisfied his appetite, he left the house, laid himself down under a tree in the green meadow, and fell asleep.

Soon afterwards, the old goat came home again from the forest. Ah, what a sight she saw. The house door stood wide open. The table, chairs, and benches were thrown down, the washing bowl lay broken to pieces, and the quilts and pillows were pulled off the bed. She sought her kids but could not find them. She called them one after another by name, but no one answered.

At last, a soft voice cried, "Dear Mother, I am in the clock case." She took her youngest kid out who told her the wolf had come and had eaten all the others. Imagine how she wept over her poor kids.

At length in her grief she went out, and the youngest kid ran with her. When they came to the meadow, there lay the wolf by the tree who snored so loud the branches shook. She gazed at him on every side and saw that something moved and struggled in his gorged belly. Ah, heavens, she thought, is it possible my poor kids whom he has swallowed down for his supper, can be still alive?

Then, the youngest kid ran home to fetch scissors, thread, and a needle for the mother goat who used them to open the wolf's stomach. Hardly had she made one cut, when one little kid thrust through. Then, when she cut farther, all six sprang out one after another and were all still alive. They had suffered no injury whatsoever, for in his greediness the wolf had swallowed them down whole.

What rejoicing there was! They embraced their dear mother and jumped like a groom at his wedding.

Then, mother said, "Now go and look for some big stones, and we will fill the beast's stomach with them while he is still asleep."

Then, the seven kids dragged the stones to her with all speed, and she stuffed many stones inside his stomach. Then, the mother sewed him up again in the greatest haste, so that he was not aware of anything and never once stirred.

When the wolf awoke from his long slumber, he stood upon his wobbly legs, and because the stones in his stomach made him very thirsty, he wanted to go to a well to drink. But as he began to walk, the stones in his stomach knocked against each other and clattered. Then cried he,

"What rumbles and tumbles
Against my poor bones?
I thought 'twas six kids,

But it feels like big stones."

And when he got to the well and stooped over the water to drink, the heavy stones made him fall in, and he drowned miserably.

When the seven kids saw what happened, they came running to the spot and cried aloud, "The wolf is dead! The wolf is dead!" and danced for joy round about the well with their mother.

The Moral:

In this tale, the enemy wolf tried to be clever and confuse the seven little goats into thinking he was their mother. The enemy has ways to trick us too and will not give up. Because we are God's children, the enemy has no power over us, yet he will try to do things to confuse us into believing the wrong way is better than the right way. We must lean on wise principles from our guardians but most importantly, follow God.

The Happily Ever After:

"The thief's purpose is to steal and kill and destroy. My purpose is to give them a rich and satisfying life." (John 10:10 NLT)

The Quest:

Thank you for your protection even when I do not know you are there. Please help us when the enemy seeks to destroy.

The Enchantment:
"Defeat is a mindset that leads to a physical loss, but an internal relationship with God leads to an external victory over your enemy."

The Once Upon A Time:
What have you learned?
Have you been in a similar situation?
How did you handle the situation?

Mirror, Mirror:
In the lines below, write one thing you can do this week to achieve a goal you have set for yourself?

____

____

____

____

DEVOTION 14: DO NOT BECOME GREEDY

The Tale: The Golden Goose

There was a man who had three sons, the youngest of whom the family considered foolish, and they often mocked him and made fun of him. Now the eldest son wanted to cut wood in the forest, and before he left home his mother prepared beautiful pancakes and a bottle of wine for him to take with him, so he might not suffer from hunger or thirst.

As he entered the forest, he met an old gray man, who bade him "Good morning," and said, "Give me a little piece of cake out of your basket and a drop of wine out of your bottle, for I am very hungry and thirsty."

But the clever son replied, "What, give you my cake and my wine? Why, if I did, I should have none for myself. Not I, indeed, so go away!" and he left the man standing and trekked on.

The young man began cutting down a tree, but soon after he made a false stroke. The axe slipped and cut his arm so badly he returned home to bind up the wound. Now, this false stroke was caused by the little old gray man.

On the next day, the second son prepared to travel into the forest to cut wood, and his mother gave him a cake and a bottle of wine. As he entered the woods, the same little old man met him, and begged for a piece of cake and a drop of wine. But the second son scoffed, "What I might give to you I shall want myself, so go away."

Then, he left the little old man standing in the road and walked on. His punishment soon came, he had scarcely given two strokes on a tree with his axe, when he hit his leg with a terrible blow and he was forced to limp home in great pain.

Now, the foolish son said to his father, "Let me go for once and cut wood in the forest."

But his father said: "No, your brothers have been hurt already, and you would do far worse because you don't understand woodcutting."

The boy, however, begged so his father said: "Go, and you will pay dearly, I expect."

His mother, however, gave him a cake which she made with water and baked in the ashes, and a bottle of sour beer.

When he reached the wood the very same little old man met him, and after greeting him kindly, said: "Give me a little of your cake and a drop from your bottle, for I am very hungry and thirsty."

"Oh," replied the simple youth, "I have only a cake, which has been baked in the ashes, and some sour beer, but I will share. Let us sit down to eat and drink together."

So, they seated themselves, and lo and behold, when the youth opened his basket, the cake had turned into a beautiful cake, and the sour beer into wine. After they had eaten and drunk enough, the little old man said, "Because you have been kindhearted, and shared your dinner with me, I will make your future lucky in all you undertake. There stands an old tree, cut it down, and you will find something good at the root."

Then the old man said "Farewell," and left him.

The youth worked hard and soon succeeded in felling the tree. Sitting at the root was a goose, whose feathers were of pure gold. He packed the goose but instead of going home, carried the bird with him to a nearby inn, where he intended to pass the night.

The landlord had three daughters, who coveted the goose with envious eyes. They had never seen such a wonderful bird and longed to have at least one of its feathers. "Ah," thought the eldest, "I shall soon have an opportunity to pluck one of them," and so it happened not long after the young man left the room. She instantly went up to the bird and took hold of its wing, but as she did so, the finger and thumb remained stuck to the feather. In a short time after, the second sister came in expecting to gain a golden feather, but as she touched her sister to move her from the bird, her hand stuck fast to her sister's dress, and neither could free herself. At last, in came the third sister with the same intention.

"Keep away, keep away!" screamed the other two. "In heaven's name, keep away!"

But she could not imagine why she should keep away. If they were near the golden bird, why should not she be there? So, she sprung forward and touched her second sister, and immediately she also was made a prisoner, and in this position they were obliged to remain by the goose all night.

In the morning, the young man came in, grabbed the goose, and went away without troubling himself about the three girls, who were following close behind him. And as he strode, they ran one behind the other, left or right of him wherever he went.

In the middle of a field, they met the parson of the parish who gawked at the procession as they drew near him. "Shame on you! What are you doing, you boldfaced tarts, running after a young man in that way through the fields? Go home, all of you."

He placed his hand on the youngest to pull her back, but the moment he touched her he also became fixed, and he was obliged to follow and run like the rest.

In a few minutes, the clerk met them, and when he saw the parson running after the girls, he wondered greatly, and cried out, "Hello, master parson, where are you running in such haste? Have you forgotten about the christening today?" And as the procession did not stop, he ran after it, and seized the parson's gown.

In a moment he found his hand affixed, and he also had to run like the rest. And now there were five trotting along, one behind the other. They trotted past two peasants holding sickles from the field. The parson begged them to come and release him and the clerk. Hardly had they touched the clerk when they also stuck fast as the others, and the simpleton with his golden goose traveled with the seven.

After a while, they entered a city in which reigned a king who had a daughter of such a melancholy disposition no one could make her laugh. Therefore, he issued a decree that whoever would make the princess laugh could have her in marriage.

Now, when the simple youth heard this, he ran before her, and the whole seven trotted after him. The moment the princess saw the ridiculous sight she burst into laughter—and they thought she would never stop.

After this, the youth approached the king and demanded his daughter in marriage according to the king's decree. But his majesty did not approve of the young man as a son in law, so the king added that before he could consent to the marriage, the youth must bring him a man who could drink all the wine in the king's cellar.

The simpleton went back into the forest, for he thought, "If anyone can help me, it is the little gray man." When he arrived at the spot where he had cut down the tree, followers in tow, a man with a very miserable expression appeared.

The youth asked him why he looked so sorrowful.

"Oh," he exclaimed, "I suffer such dreadful thirst that nothing seems able to quench it, and water I cannot endure. I have emptied a cask of wine already, but it was like a drop of liquid on a hot stone."

"I can help you," cried the young man, "come with me, and you shall have your fill, I promise you."

Upon this, he led him into the king's cellar, where the gray man opened the casks one after another and drank till his back ached. Before the day closed, he had quite emptied the king's cellar.

Again, the young man asked for his bride, but the king was annoyed at the thought of giving his daughter to such a common fellow, and to get rid of him he made another condition. He said no man should have his daughter who could not find someone able to eat up a whole mountain of bread.

Away went the simpleton back to the forest as before, and there in the same place sat a man binding himself round tightly with a belt and making the most horrible expressions. As the youth approached, he cried, "I have eaten a whole oven full of rolls, but it has not satisfied me a bit, I am as hungry as ever, and my stomach feels so empty I am obliged to bind it tightly, or I should die of hunger."

The simpleton could hardly contain himself for joy when he heard this. "Get up," he exclaimed, "and come with me, and I will give you plenty to eat, I promise."

So, he led him to the king's court, where his majesty had ordered his bakers to use all the flour in the kingdom to make bread and pile it into a huge mountain. The hungry gray man placed himself before the bread and began to eat, and before evening the whole pile had disappeared.

Then, the simpleton went a third time to the king, and asked for his bride, but the king made several excuses, and at last bargained if he could bring him a ship that could travel by land and by water, then he should, without any further conditions, marry his daughter.

The youth went at once straight to the forest and saw the same old gray man to whom he had given his cake. "Ah," he said, as the youth approached, "I sent the men to eat and drink, and I will also give you a ship that can travel by land or by sea because when you thought I was poor you were kindhearted and gave me food and drink."

The youth took the ship, and when the king saw, he was quite surprised, but he could not any longer refuse to give him his daughter in marriage. They celebrated the wedding with great pomp and after the king's death, the simple woodcutter inherited the whole kingdom and lived happily with his wife.

The Moral:
We encounter people all the time. You may never know why you met them or whether you will meet again. In this fairy tale, the three brothers all met

the same old man, yet the youngest brother treated the old man differently. The older two brothers chose not to help and left the man standing in need. The youngest brother chose to share what he had. His unselfish act led to a prosperous future for the young boy. God can increase what we have no matter how small our substance. If you give from your heart, God can bless you with more. The devil may try to defeat you, if you sow the right seeds, but God will allow them to grow. God will position you to receive the blessings He has for you.

The Enchantment:
"The only way to not have enough is to not have anything."

The Happily Ever After:
"And God will generously provide all you need. Then you will always have everything you need and plenty left over to share with others." (2 Corinthians 9:8 NLT)

The Quest:
Thank you, Lord, for the people you have put in my life that have helped me grow. . Help me to take what I have and plant seeds in others so they might grow to know you.

The Once Upon A Time:
Have you ever been in a situation where you felt like no one understood you or what you were trying to accomplish?

How did that make you feel?

What are some areas in your life where you would like to see growth?

Mirror Mirror:

Notes, takeaway, and personal reflections you gained from the lesson._______________________

____

____

____

____

____

____

____

____

____

____

____

____

____

____

____

____

DEVOTION 15: DANGERS OF ARROGANCE

The Tale: The Lion and the Gnat

Far away in Central Africa, a vast land where dense forests and wild beasts abound, the shades of night were once more descending, reminding all creatures to seek rest.

All day long the sun had perched as a great burning eye, but now, after painting the western sky with crimson, scarlet, and gold, he had disappeared into his fleecy bed while various creatures of the forest had sought their holes and resting places. The last sound had rumbled its rumble. The last bee had mumbled its mumble. The last bear had grumbled his grumble. Even the grasshoppers that chirruped all day without pause had ceased their shrill music, tucked up their long legs, and given themselves to slumber.

On a nodding grass blade, a tiny gnat had made a swinging couch. He had folded his wings, closed his tiny eyes, and had fallen asleep. Darker grew the night, and all kept still as though a powerful finger had raised up and a potent voice had whispered, "HU—SH."

When all was perfectly still, from the far away depths of the forest, like the roll of thunder came a sound, a mighty ROAR R R R!

All at once, all the beasts and birds were wide awake, and the poor gnat was nearly frightened out of his little senses, and his little heart went pit a pat. He rubbed his little eyes with his feelers, and then peered around trying to penetrate the deep gloom as he whispered in terror, "What—was—that?"

A great, big lion who, while most other denizens of the forest slept, was out hunting for prey. He came rushing and crashing through the thick undergrowth of the forest, swirling his long tail, opening wide his great jaws, and he RO AR R R ED!

The lion prowled by the spot where the little gnat hung panting at the tip of the waving grass blade. Now the little gnat was not afraid of lions, so when he saw it was only a lion, he cried out.

"Hi, stop, stop! Why are you making that horrible noise?"

The lion stopped short, then backed up to the little voice and regarded the gnat with scorn.

"Why, you tiny, little, mean, insignificant creature. How dare you speak to me?"

"How dare I speak to you?" whispered Gnat. "By the virtue of right, which is always greater than might. Why don't you keep to your own part of the forest? What right have you to disturb folks at this time of night?"

By a mighty effort the lion restrained his anger because he knew that to master others one must master oneself.

"What right?" Lion repeated in dignified tones. "Because I'm King of the Forest. That's why. I can do no wrong, for all the other creatures of the forest are afraid of me. I do what I please, I say what I please, I eat whom I please, I go where I please—simply because I'm King of the Forest."

"But who told you that you were king?" demanded Gnat. "Just answer me that."

"Who told me! Why, everyone acknowledges it—didn't I tell you that everyone is afraid of me?"

"Indeed! But don't say all, for I'm not afraid of you. And further, I deny your right to be king."

The lion worked himself into a perfect fury.

"You—you—YOU deny my right as king?"

"I do, and what is more, you shall never be king until you have fought and conquered me."

The lion laughed a great lion laugh, which was not the laugh of a mere cat.

"Fight—did you say fight? Who ever heard of a lion fighting a gnat? Go, out of my way, you atom of nothing. I'll blow you to the other end of the world."

But though the lion puffed his cheeks like great bellows and blew with all his might, he could not disturb the little gnat's hold on the swaying grass blade.

"You'll blow all your whiskers away if you are not careful," The gnat laughed. "but you won't move me. And if you dare leave this spot without fighting me, I'll tell all the beasts of the forest you are afraid of me, and they'll make me king."

"Ho, ho!" roared Lion. "Very well, since you will fight, let it be so."

"You agree to the conditions, then? The one who conquers shall be king?"

"Oh, certainly," laughed Lion, for he expected an easy victory. "Are you ready?"

"Quite ready."

"Then—GO!" He sprang forward with open jaws, thinking he could easily swallow a million gnats. But just as the great jaws were about to close upon the blade of grass whereto the gnat clung, what should happen but the gnat spread his wings and nimbly flew right into one of Lion's nostrils. And there he began to sting, sting, sting. Lion wondered, and thundered, and blundered—but Gnat went on stinging while Lion foamed, and moaned, and groaned. Yet, still the gnat stung. Lion rubbed his head on the ground in agony. He swirled his tail in furious passion. He roared. He spluttered. He sniffed. He snuffed—but Gnat did not give up.

"O my poor nose, my nose, my nose!" said Lion. "Come down, come down, come down! My nose, my nose, my nose! You're King of the Forest, you're the king, you're the king—only come down. My nose, my nose, my nose!"

So at last, Gnat flew out from Lion's nostril and returned to his waving grass blade, while the lion slunk away into the depths of the forest with his tail between his legs—beaten by a tiny gnat.

"What a fine fellow am I, to be sure!" said Gnat, as he proudly plumed his wings. "I've beaten a lion—a lion! Dear me, I ought to have been king long ago. I'm so clever, so big, so strong—oh! ..."

Gnat cried because he found himself entangled in some silky threads. While gloating over his victory, the wind had risen, and his grass blade had swayed to and fro while a gust bent the blade to the ground and into a spider's web. O how the victorious gnat struggled to be free. Alas! he became more entangled than ever. Then—flipperty flopperty, flipperty flopperty, flop, flip, flop—down his stairs came the cunning spider and quickly gobbled up the little gnat for his supper, and that was the end of him.

The Moral:

In this fairy tale, the odds were stacked against the gnat because he was small and not known for being a fighter. On the other hand, all the jungle animals feared the lion, so he felt losing was impossible against the gnat. The gnat, although small, was smart and knew his capabilities. The gnat worked with what God gave him to defeat the lion. God created us and gave us many qualities that make us special. But after defeating the lion, the gnat boasted and became proud. As a result, he found himself in another fight only this time he was the loser, not the winner. We must remain humble in the Lord. God grants victory and fights for his people.

The Happily Ever After:
"Pride leads to disgrace, but with humility comes wisdom." (Proverbs 11:2 NLT)

The Quest:
In all situations and circumstances, give me a spirit of humility so that I do not become boastful or more than I am for all that I have and do is because of you God.

The Enchantment:
"It matters not the external size of the fighter, but the internal humility of the fighter."

The Once Upon A Time:
What have you learned?
Have you been in a similar situation?
How did you handle the situation?

Mirror, Mirror:
Notes, takeaway, and personal reflections you gained from the lesson. ______________________

____

____

____

____

____

____

———————————————————————

———————————————————————

———————————————————————

———————————————————————

———————————————————————

———————————————————————

———————————————————————

———————————————————————

DEVOTION 16: BE THANKFUL FOR THE THINGS YOU DO HAVE

The Tale: The Travelers and Plane Tree

Two travelers walked along a bare and dusty road in the heat of a summer's day. Coming presently to a Plane tree, they joyfully turned aside to shelter from the burning rays of the sun in the deep shade of its spreading branches. As they rested, looking up into the tree, one of them remarked to his companion, "What a useless tree the Plane is! It bears no fruit and is of no service to man at all." The Plane tree interrupted him with indignation. "You ungrateful creature!" it cried: "you come and take shelter under me from the scorching sun, and then, in the very act of enjoying the cool shade of my foliage, you abuse me and call me good for nothing."

The Moral:
In this fairy tale, the travelers found shelter from the heat at the foot of a tree. Though the tree was providing much needed help from the burning sun

through its shade, it was not enough. On a hot day when the sun beats down on you, sitting under a tree brings relief. However, the traveler felt the shade was not sufficient. The traveler expected the tree to produce food. The moral of the story is in all things we must be grateful. Being ungrateful is not a good characteristic to have. We need to be thankful for the things we have and realize all our blessings even in times when it appears we may not get what we want. The traveler was ungrateful because his focus was on what was not provided by the tree and he overlooked what the tree did provide.

The Happily Ever After:

"Be thankful in all circumstances, for this is God's will for you who belong to Christ Jesus." (1 Thessalonians 5:18 NLT)

The Quest:

Lord, thank you for all the things you provide for me.

The Enchantment:

"Having more does not change a person that values having none."

The Once Upon A Time:

What have you learned?
Have you been in a similar situation?
How did you handle the situation?

Mirror, Mirror:

In the lines below, write one thing you can do this week to achieve a goal you have set for yourself?

____

____

____

____

____

____

____

____

____

____

____

PRINCESS
RULES

DEVOTION 17: ENTERTAINING STRANGERS

The Tale: The Princess and the Pea

Once upon a time, a prince wanted a princess—a real princess. He traveled the world searching for one but discovering whether they were real was quite difficult because something was often not right about them. Finally, he returned home, and he was very sad because he wanted a real princess.

One stormy night, the sky poured rain down in torrents. In the middle of the thunderous storm someone knocked at the town gate, and the old king sent for someone to open it.

A princess stood outside, sopping wet from the rain. Water streamed from her hair, her clothes, and her lovely lady shoes. But she claimed she was a real princess.

"Well we shall soon see," thought the old queen.

She prepared the lady's bedroom, took all the bed clothes off and laid a pea on the bedframe. Then, she sent her servants to pile twenty mattresses on top of the pea, and then twenty feather beds on top of the mattresses. This was where the princess was to sleep that night. In the morning, they asked her how she slept.

"Oh, terribly bad!" said the princess. "I have hardly closed my eyes the whole night! Heaven knows what was in the bed. I seemed to be lying upon some hard thing, and my whole body is black and blue this morning. It is terrible!"

They saw at once she must be a real princess when she had felt the pea through twenty mattresses and twenty feather beds. Nobody but a real princess could have such delicate skin.

So, the prince took her to be his wife because he was sure he had found a real princess, and the pea was put into a museum, where it can still be seen if no one has stolen it.

The Moral:

People often turn others away because of their race, ethnicity, or how they look. There are certainly some people in the world whom we must test to ensure they are good. As you think about this, how would the story have ended if the king had not sent for the door to be open? What would have happened if the princess was turned away because of how she looked? Would there have been a happily ever after for her or the prince?

The Happily Ever After:

"Look! I stand at the door and knock. If you hear my voice and open the door, I will come in, and we will share a meal together as friends." (Revelation 3:20 NLT)

The Quest:
Lord, thank you for the doors you open and even for the ones you close. When you knock give me the will to open and receive the blessings you have in store for me. Amen.

The Enchantment:
"The fastest way to learn a life lesson is to fall, the more you fall the more you learn."

The Once Upon A Time:
When you fall down in life, do you call on God?
Can you think of a time when things didn't work out like you'd hoped?
What did you learn?

Mirror, Mirror:
In the lines below, write about a time when you felt broken. ___________________________________

____

____

____

____

____

____

MR. Dr.
CROAK

DEVOTION 18: NOT EVERYONE IS WHO THEY SAY THEY ARE

The Tale: The Quack Frog

Once upon a time a frog came forth from his home in the marshes and proclaimed to all the world that he was a learned physician skilled in medicine and able to cure all diseases.

Among the crowd was a fox who called out, "You, a doctor? Why, how can you heal others when you cannot even cure your own lame legs and blotched, wrinkled skin?"

The Moral:

If you want to be a leader you must be willing to do as you say. In this tale, the fox questions the frog because his appearance did not match his words. The frog portrayed himself as someone he was not. Why would anyone want to follow a hypocrite? If we want people to follow us, we must be willing to follow our own example. In addition, if we want to follow someone, we should make sure they do what they say. Jesus is the greatest example of a leader whom we should follow.

The Happily Ever After:
"Trust in the LORD with all your heart; do not depend on your own understanding." (Proverbs 3:5 NLT)

The Quest:
As people cross my path, Lord I ask you to give me insight as to who is a friend or foe.
The Enchantment:
"You can't expect people to follow you if you're not willing to follow your own lead."

The Once Upon a Time:
What have you learned?
Have you been in a similar situation?
How did you handle the situation?

Mirror, Mirror:
Notes, takeaway, and personal reflections you gained from the lesson/

Mr. Dr.
CROAK

DEVOTION 19: FOLLOW THE LEADER

The Tale: The Crab and His Mother

An old crab said to her son, "Why do you walk sideways, my son? You ought to walk straight."

The young crab replied, "Show me how, dear mother, and I'll follow your example."

The old crab tried, but tried in vain, and then saw how foolish she had been to find fault with her child.

The Moral:
Setting the right example is important because people always watch what we do. The little crab copied his mother. The mother crab did not realize that her baby crab walked the same way she walked. Strive to do the right thing. Then those who watch you may follow your pattern. What example are you setting? Setting a good example helps others to want to follow.

The Happily Ever After:
"Dear brothers and sisters, pattern your lives after mine, and learn from those who follow our example." (Philippians 3:17 NLT)

The Quest:
God, thank you for being the greatest example of how to grow and live in an imperfect world.

The Enchantment:
"No one wants to set a bad example. Christ set a notable example for us to follow by always doing the right thing."

The Once Upon a Time:
What have you learned?
Have you been in a similar situation?
How did you handle the situation?

Mirror, Mirror:
Notes, takeaway, and personal reflections you gained from the lesson.

____

____

____

____

____

____

____

____

____

____

DEVOTION 20: KEEP YOUR EYES OPEN

The Tale: The Lion and the Fox

A certain lion was growing incredibly old. He struggled to catch his prey. Then, one day he had an idea. He would stay in his cave and catch and eat any animal that came near him. Not long after this a foolish rabbit came hopping along. When he neared the cave he saw the old lion lying there. "How are you today, Mr. Lion?" he asked politely. "Oh!" said Mr. Lion. "I am so sick. Please come in and feel how hot my head is." The foolish rabbit went into the cave. No sooner had he reached out his paw to feel how hot the lion's head was when snap snap—and that was the end of the foolish rabbit.

Then, a foolish sheep came wandering along. When he came to the cave, he saw the old lion lying there. "How are you today, Mr. Lion?" he asked politely. "Oh!" said Mr. Lion. "I am so sick. Please come in and feel how hot my head is." The foolish sheep went into the cave. No sooner had he reached out his foot to feel how hot the lion's head was when snap snap—and that was the end of the foolish sheep.

The next day a fox came trotting along. When he came near to the cave, he saw the old lion lying there.

"How are you today, Mr. Lion." he asked politely. "Oh!" said Mr Lion. "I am so sick. Please come in and feel how hot my head is." The wise fox was cautious because he had noticed that all his friends who went to see the old lion did not come back.

He came close enough to talk to the lion, but he did not go into the cave.

"Please come right in, and feel how hot my head is," said Mr. Lion again.

"Oh no! Mr. Lion," said the fox. "I can see many footprints going into your cave, but none come out. You are dangerous, Mr. Lion. Goodbye!" And the fox ran off as fast as he could.

The Moral:
Do not be quick to accept invitations without knowing what you are accepting. Some people seek to destroy you for their gain. Just like the lion, enemies will invite you in only for you to find out that you have been invited into a bad situation. With God we do not have to be afraid. The fox did not fear, but he used his mind to observe what was going on.

The Happily Ever After:
"For God has not given us a spirit of fear and timidity, but of power, love, and self-discipline." (2 Timothy 1:7 NLT)

The Quest:
Keep my eyes and my mind clear so that I can see what lies in front of me.

The Enchantment:
"Without God, your eyes only see what is in front of you because you are limited to the physical."

The Once Upon A Time:
What have you learned?
Have you been in a similar situation?
How did you handle the situation?

Mirror, Mirror:
Notes, takeaway, and personal reflections you gained from the lesson. ___________________

____

____

____

____

____

____

____

____

____

____

DEVOTION 21: RESPECT OTHER'S PROPERTY

The Tale: Goldilocks and the Three Bears

Once upon a time, there was a little girl named Goldilocks. She went for a walk in the forest. Soon, she came upon a house. She knocked, and when no one answered, she walked right in.

At the table in the kitchen, there were three bowls of porridge. Goldilocks was hungry. She tasted the porridge from the first bowl.

"This porridge is too hot!" she said.

She tasted the porridge from the second bowl.

"This porridge is too cold," she said.

She tasted the last bowl of porridge.

"Ahhh, this porridge is just right," she said, and she ate it all up.

After she'd eaten three breakfasts belonging to the bears, she decided she was feeling a little tired. So, she walked into the living room where she saw three chairs. Goldilocks sat in the first chair to rest.

"This chair is too big!" she said.

She sat in the second chair.

"This chair is too big, too!" she said.

She tried the last and smallest chair.

"Ahhh, this chair is just right." She sighed, but just as she settled down into the chair to rest, it broke into pieces.

Goldilocks was very tired by this time, she went upstairs to the bedroom. She lay down in the first bed, but it was too hard. Then, she lay in the second bed, but it was too soft. Then, she lay down in the third bed—and it was just right. Goldilocks fell asleep.

As she was sleeping, the three bears came home.

"Someone's been eating my porridge," growled Papa bear.

"Someone's been eating my porridge," said Mama bear.

"Someone's been eating my porridge and they ate it all up!" cried Baby bear.

"Someone's been sitting in my chair," growled Papa bear.

"Someone's been sitting in my chair," said Mama bear.

"Someone's been sitting in my chair and they've broken it to pieces," cried Baby bear.

They decided to search their house and when they got upstairs to the bedroom, Papa bear growled,

"Someone's been sleeping in my bed."

"Someone's been sleeping in my bed, too" said Mama bear.

"Someone's been sleeping in my bed and she's still there!" exclaimed Baby bear.

Just then, Goldilocks woke up. When she saw the three bears, she screamed, "Help!"

Then, she jumped up, ran out of the room, down the stairs, opened the door, and dashed away into the forest. She never returned to the home of the three bears.

The Moral:

Respecting others will have a good impact on our future. Goldilocks entered a house owned by bears while they were away. Not only did she enter, but she made herself at home. This was wrong and we must learn to respect others and their property. If we do wrong, we will not get away with it. Imagine how the bears felt. We may not know how our actions affect someone else's life, but we would not like someone to mess up our things.

The Happily Ever After:

"Instead, be kind to each other, tenderhearted, forgiving one another just as God through Christ has forgiven you." (Ephesians 4:32 NLT)

The Quest:

Thank you, Lord for all the things you have given to me. Bless that do not have or are less fortunate. Let me not forget all things come from you.

The Enchantment:
"Nothing is really worth having if you don't work for it. It's the work that gives the purpose and meaning."

The Once Upon A Time:
What have you learned?
Have you been in a similar situation?
How did you handle the situation?

Mirror, Mirror:
Notes, takeaway, and personal reflections you gained from the lesson. ___________________

____

____

____

____

____

____

____

____

____

____

____

____

____

____

____

____

____

____

____

____

DEVOTION 22: BE SATISFIED WITH WHAT YOU HAVE

The Tale: The Dog and His Reflection

A dog, to whom a butcher had thrown a bone, was hurrying home with his prize as fast as he could go. As he crossed a narrow footbridge, he gazed down and saw his reflection in the water. But the dog thought he saw a real dog carrying a bone much bigger than his own. At once, he dropped his bone and sprang at the dog in the river, only to find himself swimming for his dear life to reach the shore. At last, he managed to scramble out, and as the greedy dog whimpered thinking about the good bone he had lost, he realized his error.

The Moral:
Be thankful for what you have. God has given each of us something and we must be content with what we have. Contentment does not mean that we do not work or aspire to become more. Greed is wanting more because we see more when we already have

enough. Greed can cause us to end up with nothing. Like the dog in this tale who chased after something he already possessed, do not allow your wants to overshadow your needs.

The Happily Ever After:
"Not that I was ever in need, for I have learned how to be content with whatever I have." (Philippians 4:11 NLT)

The Quest:
I may not have it all but thank you God for what you have given me. I am grateful because you did not have to give.

The Enchantment:
"Trying to gain more than enough can lead to a loss of where you started."

The Once Upon A Time:
What have you learned?
Have you been in a similar situation?
How did you handle the situation?

Mirror, Mirror:
Notes, takeaway, and personal reflections you gained from the lesson. _______________________
____
____

ABOUT THE AUTHOR

Antwan L. Houser Sr. is an humble and dedicated leader and pastor who loves working with and impacting the lives of youth and young adults in all facets of life.

Antwan has always had a thirst and desire to work in and be a community leader. He began to make his mark on the community when God called him to the ministry. With dedication and drive, that work continues today.

Committed to being an advocate of change and improving the quality of life, he founded and is the president of UPLIFT (United Pastors & Leaders Influencing Future Transformations), an organization with the mission of coming together with the common goal of influencing youth to be an impact of transformation, transforming their futures along with their communities. Under UPLIFT a boys' and girls' mentoring program was also founded.

Antwan speaks around the world in grade schools, colleges and universities, churches, and for other nonprofits hoping to motivate, inspire, and encourage.

He is also a decorated United States Navy veteran, a member of Kappa Alpha Psi Fraternity Incorporated, a member of the Indianapolis Urban League, and a member of the Indiana Rotary Club. He is married with three children. He is a college graduate who has achieved five degrees including an Associates, two Bachelors, and two Masters.

Antwan was a 2015 recipient of the Mayor's Community Service Award for the State of Indiana awarded by Mayor Greg Ballard. He was also the recipient of a Letter of Appreciation for his community service and service on Martin Luther King Jr. Day, awarded by Congressman André Carson. He is a man who lives by his life's Scripture "to whom much is given, much is required."